S0-BAF-626

A10

MEET ALL THESE FRIENDS IN BUZZ BOOKS:

Thomas the Tank Engine
The Animals of Farthing Wood
Biker Mice From Mars
James Bond Junior
Joshua Jones
Fireman Sam
Rupert
Babar

First published in Great Britain in 1994
by Buzz Books
an imprint of Reed Children's Books
Michelin House, 81 Fulham Road, London SW3 6RB
and Auckland, Melbourne, Singapore and Toronto

ISBN 1 85591 369 0

Printed in Italy by Olivotto

A MOUSE
AND HIS
MOTORCYCLE

Story by Norman Redfern
Illustrations by Arkadia

The planet Plutark had been wrecked by its greedy citizens. There was nothing left – no food, no water, no oil.

So they began plundering other planets. Lawrence Limburger landed on Earth. His disguise: a business suit. His mission: to dig up the planet, and ship it all back to Plutark!

Late one night, Limburger stood on the roof of his office block and looked down on Chicago. In his hand was a metal can.

"This one little canister contains enough knockout gas to send the whole of Chicago to sleep for twenty-four hours," he told his henchmen.

"So goodnight, citizens, and pleasant dreams," he whispered over the edge, "because by the time you awaken, there will be no more Chicago!"

Limburger and his gang pulled on their gas-masks. He laughed as the canister dropped towards the city below. Then he

8

heard something that made him scowl.

From the roof of a nearby building came
the roar of motorcycle engines. The Biker
Mice From Mars were on their way!

They raced down the side of the building
and slammed into the street. Throttle and
Vinnie blocked the road with their bikes.

Cars skidded to a halt as Modo landed in the open space below the Limburger Tower.

The canister was about to hit the ground when Modo flung his metal arm up and caught it.

"Game over!" shouted Throttle. "Let's hit the highway, bro's!"

Up on the roof, Limburger was furious.

"Get those vexatious vermin!" he screamed. "I want that canister back!"

But the Biker Mice were nowhere to be seen.

11

Limburger stormed into Karbunkle's laboratory.

"Show me something truly nasty," he said. "Something that will rid me of those miserable Mice!"

Karbunkle held up a test-tube full of horrible blue slime.

"Forget the Mice," replied Karbunkle. "Here's my latest invention – Toxic Goo!

It eats through anything. Spill some in the
park. It'll make a very nasty mess!"

"But I don't want a nasty mess," said
Limburger angrily. "It will do me no good
on Plutark!"

Karbunkle pointed to a large drum of
white powder. "If you sprinkle some of that
special powder on the ground, it will return
to normal again," he said.

"Excellent," nodded Limburger. "I have a plan. Somebody spills the Toxic Goo. I, of course, volunteer to clean up the mess."

"Then you just sprinkle on the magic powder," said Karbunkle, "and hey presto! Perfect Earth land, to dig up and send home to Plutark!"

"By the way," said Limburger, "I wonder what Toxic Goo does to Mice… "

Modo loved his bike. He tuned it, cleaned
it and polished it until it was perfect in
every way.

It was a warm summer's day in the park.
Vinnie and Throttle lazed on the riverbank.
Charley was swimming in the cool clear
water. Modo was polishing his bike. High
overhead, a helicopter buzzed.

Suddenly, a turbo barge swept up the river. It was heavily laden with vats full of nasty-looking blue slime.

"Check out the Captain!" yelled Modo. "It's old oil-slick himself – Greasepit! I'm gonna find out what he's up to!"

Modo kick-started his bike and roared up the riverbank until he was level with the ship. Greasepit spotted him.

16

"Hey, Mousie!" he sneered. "You's about to get da blues!"

He spun the wheel and the barge lurched towards the shore. With a horrible crunch, it rammed the bank, and its cargo rolled off the deck into the park.

Modo watched in horror as the Toxic Goo spilled over the grass. Another drum burst, and a wave of blue slime swept over him.

He felt it eat away at his clothes and his fur. Then it oozed towards his bike. "Hang on, bike," he cried. "I'm a-comin' to save you!"

Throttle and Vinnie roared up.

"Get out of that goo, bro'!" said Throttle. "It's crime slime!"

"But…my bike!" cried Modo.

Suddenly, the distant buzz of the
helicopter grew louder. A rope dropped out
of the sky, and a clamp gripped Modo's
motorcycle. As the helicopter winched the
bike away, Limburger's voice drifted down.

"Not your bike," he taunted, "my bike!"

19

Back at their base, Charley wiped the Toxic Goo off Modo. He was weak. The slime had sapped his strength.

"My bike," he moaned. "Limburger's got my bike!"

"We'll get it back, bro'!" promised Vinnie. "Biker's honour! Charley's got a plan."

"But it's a dangerous plan," Charley warned him.

20

"That's why I like it," grinned Vinnie.

Charley had attached Limburger's sleeping-gas canister to Vinnie's bike. She had also fitted a new supercharger.

"It will give you thirty seconds of supersonic speed, no more," she told him.

"That's all I'll need," said Vinnie.

The Limburger Tower was surrounded by Plutarkian guards. The Biker Mice and Charley watched as Greasepit led an army of diggers off to destroy the ruined park.

"Hurry up," said Charley, "before the city's best park takes a one-way ride to Plutark!"

"You got it," said Vinnie. "Blast off!"

With his helmet set to deep space mode, Vinnie roared towards the building. His bike screamed past the guards, faster than the speed of sound.

Once inside, he hit a button and the knockout gas began seeping out. Limburger's guards slumped to the floor, fast asleep.

Outside, Charley checked her stopwatch.

"Time's up," she said. "Now it's up to you two!"

Throttle and Modo set off on Throttle's bike. They raced past the sleeping guards, roared up the stairs and skidded into Karbunkle's laboratory.

Limburger and Karbunkle were wide awake. They had been wearing gas masks! Modo's bike was chained to the floor. Karbunkle was leaning over it with a glowing blowtorch.

Modo aimed his arm-cannon and fired. The chains shattered. His bike was free!

"Go get 'em, little darlin'!" he shouted.

The bike roared into action, lights blazing. It fired a rocket which grazed Karbunkle's nose before blasting a hole in the wall.

"Emergency exit," yelled Limburger. "Follow me!"

Limburger and Karbunkle leapt through the hole in the wall. There was a long silence. Then a loud splash. They had landed in the fountain, hundreds of feet below!

Modo threw his arms round his bike.

"That's my bike!" he said.

"But we still have to do something about Greasepit and the Toxic Goo," said Throttle.

Suddenly, Modo's motorcycle spun round. It aimed its headlight at Karbunkle's drum of magic powder.

"I don't believe it!" said Throttle.

"'Evaporating Powder – Destroys Toxic Goo!'"

Modo patted his bike.

"I told ya," he grinned, "she's the best!"

Throttle grinned. He grabbed a jar of

powder and jumped back on his bike.

"Time to save the park, bro's," he said. "Everyone ready?"

Modo turned to his bike. Its horn beeped and its headlight flashed.

"Then let's rock – and ride!"